♥

This book belongs to

Anthony Raymond

An Imprint of Sterling Publishing
387 Park Avenue South
New York, NY 10016

ISBN 978-1-4351-4765-2

www.humphreys-corner.com

Adapted from Humphrey's Bedtime
First published in 2000 by The Penguin Group

Manufactured in China
Lot#:
2 4 6 8 10 9 7 5 3 1
06/13

Humphrey's Bedtime

Sally Hunter

It was Baby Jack's bedtime...
Humphrey and Lottie tucked him in.
"Night night, sleep tight".

Baby Jack had to go first because he was the smallest.
Next it was Humphrey's bedtime...

But Lottie said, "I am allowed to stay up very, very late.
That's because I'm the biggest."

Humphrey got his toys all ready for bathtime.

He made big bubble mountains...

and magic potions.
Humphrey had a lovely time.

But Lottie wasn't getting ready for bed.
She said her babies needed a really good wash!

"Pajamas on, Humphrey."

Humphrey had hot milk and buttery toast.

He felt warm and cozy in his tummy.

Mop liked his, too.

But Lottie didn't have time for dinner!
She said, "oh no...my babies are having tea.
Eat it all up and you will grow big and strong."

Humphrey had a horsey ride!

'Neigh... Neigghh... Up the wooden hill to Bed.'

Humphrey had fun seeing how high he could fly.
Mommy said, "I think it's storytime now!"

It was Humphrey's best book.

"once upon a time, there lived a little pixie
at the bottom of the yard..."

He was all snuggly...and sleepy.

Humphrey didn't quite hear how the pixie and his friends lived happily ever after because he fell asleep before the end.

Ssssh. Night night, Little Humphrey. x

But Lottie still wasn't getting ready for bed!
She was having problems with her babies.

Lulu was being silly...

Trevor wouldn't get ready for bed properly...

Barry wouldn't lie down...

and Bear had gotten lost.

Lottie felt all hot...

and CROSS!

Dad came in from work. "What's all this..?"
he said. "Come on, my funny little girl."

"Off we go...

"...to bed."

Night Night
Baby Jack, Humphrey and Lottie.
Sweet Dreams. x